THE CRANKY BLUE CRAB

A tale in verse

DAWN L. WATKINS
ILLUSTRATED BY TIM DAVIS

journeyforth®

Greenville, South Carolina

Library of Congress Cataloging-in-Publication Data

Watkins, Dawn L.
    The cranky blue crab / by Dawn L Watkins : illustrated by
Timothy N. Davis.

Summary: Bored with living by the edge of the sea, Crusty
the Crab decides to try living on land.

    ISBN 0-89084-506-9
    [1. Crabs-Fiction.   2. Stories in rhyme.]   1. Davis, Timothy N.,
ill. I I. Title.
PZ8.3.W248Cr   1990
[E]-dc20   89-28060
                                                  CIP
                                                   AC

The Cranky Blue Crab

Edited by Anne Smith

© 1990 BJU Press
Greenville, SC 29609
JourneyForth Books is a division of BJU Press.

ISBN 978-0-89084-506-6

20   19   18   17   16   15   14   13   12   11   10

for Andrew

Down by the sea,
By its rippling edge,
Lived Crusty the Crab
Under Jaggedy Ledge.
His claws were bright blue;
Bright red were the tips—
Sun-burned, some said,
From his waving at ships.

Every ship that he saw
From the crest of a wave
Looked better to him
Than his water-worn cave.
When the sun shone too hot
On his back he complained,
But he never was pleased
Whenever it rained.

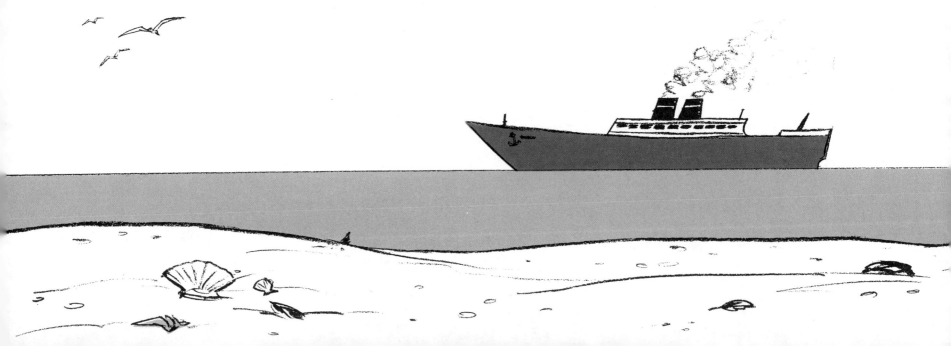

One day the tide
Was at a new low;
Crusty said to the squid,
"I really should go.
I'm bored with this place
And its limited range.
I think I'll live out
On the land for a change."

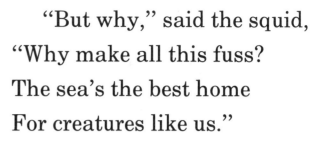

"But why," said the squid,
"Why make all this fuss?
The sea's the best home
For creatures like us."

"Maybe for you—
Not me," said the crab;
"Life in this cave
Is unbearably drab."

He stretched out his claws
And gave a great yawn.
Then he got himself up,
And he got himself gone.

The tide rolled him out
On a wide sandy shore
With an ungentle push
And an unfriendly roar.
He climbed over beams
Of small rotting hulls.
Whenever he rested,
He was swooped by the gulls.

They dived for his shell;
They skimmed past his eyes.
"Look, look," they all cried,
"What a tasty surprise!"

Crusty shook a blue claw
As a threat most absurd.
"Stay out of my way,
You cantankerous birds!"

The gulls only laughed
And went wheeling away—
Then swooped him once more
Just to see what he'd say.
    At the top of the ridge
Crusty met his first flea.
"And who," said the crab,
"Might this creature be?"

The flea tipped his head,
Tapped one of his feet—
"I'm the cleverest flea
That you'll ever meet."
    Crusty backed up a bit
And peered from his shell.
"You're surely the boldest
From what I can tell!"

The flea looked him over,
Then said with a grin—
"From the looks of you, sir,
We just might be kin."

Crusty thought this unlikely,
But he let it pass.
He went over the ridge
And out on green grass.

Behind him came Flea
In a leap and a bound.
"If you're new in these parts,
Let me show you around."

"Very well," said the crab,
"But don't slow me down.
I'm on an adventure."
And he frowned a crab frown.

"Well, I like adventure,"
Said the jovial flea,
"I know where to find it,
So just follow me."

"Do you have a name?"
Asked Crusty quite coolly.

Said the flea with a flourish,
"'Tis Fleabus O'Tooly.
And yours, my good fellow?
Your name, if you will."

But Crusty was puffing
To get up the hill.

"Do you not have a name?"
Asked Flea with surprise.

The crab stared at Flea
With his periscope eyes.

"Of course, I've a name,
You ridiculous flea.
I'm Crusty the Crab
From the edge of the sea."

   "That's better," said Flea,
"Now we'll get along fine.
Let's trade this salt air
For the scent of the pine."

   So off the two went
Away from sea's edge,
Across a wide meadow
Toward a dark hedge.

A bright beetle hailed them
As they went along.
"Hello, my friend Flea,
Want to hear a new song?"

"Who is this?" asked the crab,
His antennae knit.
"I don't want to stop here,
Not one little bit!"

"Oh, Beetle's all right,"
Said Flea with a smile.
"And it might do you good
To rest for a while."

The crab didn't like it,
But they stopped for a visit.
"This song," asked the Flea,
"What kind of song is it?"

"A song of the meadow,"
Said Beetle with pleasure.
"I wrote it myself.
Let me sing the first measure."
    Beetle thrummed his hard wings,
With snib-ticklety-click.
    "This," said the crab,
"Is no song. It's a trick!"
    "Shhhh," warned the flea,
"Can't you be more polite?
What kind of a song
Did you ever write?"
    Crusty said, "Ump harumph.
When I'm falling asleep,
I have often heard whales
Singing songs of the deep."

"Well, this is the meadow,
And the way Beetle sings
Is the way that we like it—
You remember these things."

Then Crusty was quiet
'Til the music was done.
"That was all very nice,
But I really must run."

"Where are you going?"
Asked Beetle Brightknee.
"I might go along
If you all would invite me."

Before Crusty answered,
The flea said, "Why sure.
We could use a musician
To enliven this tour."

Crusty sighed to himself,
But he made no complaint.
If no other thing,
He was learning restraint.

Across the rich meadow
Came a winging of color;
So bright was the creature
It made flowers seem duller.
It settled at last
On a thistle near Crusty;

Its wings were deep purple,
And just slightly dusty.
    "Hi, Flutterby,"
Said Beetle Brightknee.
    "Good day to you, Wings,"
Said the good-natured flea.

Then Crusty's blue shell
Turned to pink with the shock.
"A princess comes here,
And just hear how they talk!
No one should speak
To a princess that way."

All this he thought—
And thought not to say.
"Hello," said the purple
And gold bedecked thing,
And ever so gracefully
Dipped her one wing.

It occurred to the crab
That he'd like to bow,
And then he remembered
He'd never learned how.

"This is a crab,"
Flea told Flutterby.
"He's on an adventure,
But didn't say why."

Flutterby said
In a voice like a song,
"He doesn't have to.
May I come along?"

"Yes, yes," said the beetle.
"Please do," said the flea.
Crusty smiled his first smile
Since he'd left the sea.

Three of them walked,
And one of them flew;
Together they made
One huzbumbley crew.

When they got near the hedge,
They heard a low buzz;
Crusty had no idea
Of what the buzz was.

It started out soft
Like a grandmother's hum,
And then it got loud
Like a big engine thrum.

Beetle crouched down,
And Flea hopped away.
Crusty stood listening,
Unhinged with dismay.
Down on the crab zoomed
A huge swarm of bees
And set him to knocking
All eight of his knees.

"EEYIEE!" hollered Crusty,
His claws on his head—
Which was the worst thing
For they shone blue and red.

"Oh, wait," said Flutterby,
"Please wait, if you will."
At the sound of her voice,
The bees hovered still.

"This is no flower
Though the colors seem right.
This crab is our guest—
And you gave him a fright."

When they heard Flutterby,
The bees backed away;
You may always believe
What the butterflies say.

"That was close," said the beetle.
"Sure was," said the flea.
"Oh, pah," said the crab,
"They didn't scare me."

"Shall I call them back?"
The butterfly said.
"Oh, don't bother," said he,
"Let them go on ahead."

Flea winked at Beetle,
And Flutterby flitted.
Crusty thought no one saw
That he'd been outwitted.

    On they all went,
With the day growing hot.

    "Our terrain," said Crusty,
"Is not like you've got."

    "This is Sea Meadow"
Said Beetle Brightknee.

    "Sand's better," said Crab,
"If you care to ask me."

"Nobody does," said Flea,
As he climbed up a stone.
    With crossed claws said Crusty,
"I will go on alone!"
    "Now, wait," said Flutterby.
    "Go ahead," said the flea.
    "It's not safe," said Beetle,
"For one from the sea."
    "I'm going," said Crusty,
And left in a huff.
    "Let him go," said the flea,
"I've quite had enough."
    "Be kind," said Flutterby,
"Let's follow a while."
And she won the flea over
With her wonderful smile.

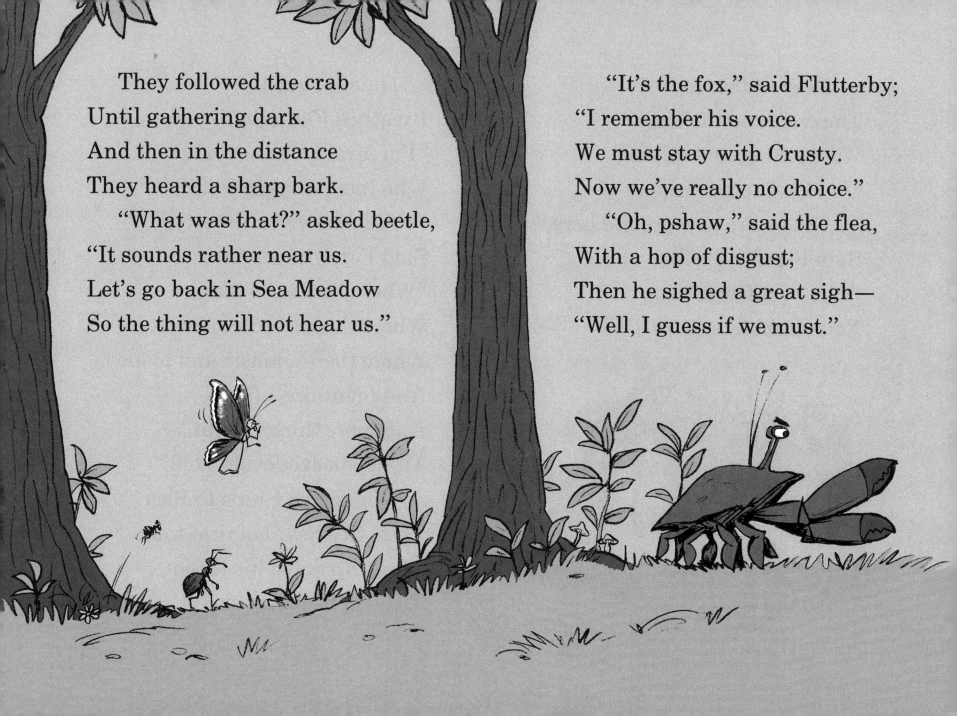

They followed the crab
Until gathering dark.
And then in the distance
They heard a sharp bark.

"What was that?" asked beetle,
"It sounds rather near us.
Let's go back in Sea Meadow
So the thing will not hear us."

"It's the fox," said Flutterby;
"I remember his voice.
We must stay with Crusty.
Now we've really no choice."

"Oh, pshaw," said the flea,
With a hop of disgust;
Then he sighed a great sigh—
"Well, I guess if we must."

Deep in the thicket
The crab and the fox
Were sitting and talking
On top of some rocks.

   "So you're new around here,"
Said Finefur the Sly.
"I know a few things
You might like to try."

Quietly, quietly
Breathed Flutterby,
"I'm afraid it's the fox
Who has things to try."

   "I'll show you the city,"
Said Fox with a wink,
"Where lights are like stars;
Where there's soda to drink;
Where there's music and money,
And fountains of gold,
And more things to eat
Than you ever could hold."

   Whispered Beetle to Flea,
"Yes, I've heard of that tour;
It's a trip down his throat,
You can be pretty sure."

"Let's go," said the crab,
"That city's for me.
No more dull life
At the edge of the sea."

    "So you've come from Seashore;
You've come a long way."

    "I've walked half a mile
Since early today."

"Where are my manners?"
Asked Fox, grinning wide.
"You go to sleep,
And I'll give you a ride."

    "Uh oh," said Beetle,
With fear in his eyes.
"But what can we do
To a fox of that size?"

Then in a flash
The fox made a leap
And snatched the crab up
In his gleaming white teeth.
  "Avaunt!" cried Flea
Like a knight on a charger.
And he sailed against Fox
Who was ninety times larger.
He grabbed Fox's tail
And bit down like a vice.
Fox sprang off the ground
And rolled over twice.
He fell back to earth
And let out a wail.
Then he scrambled around
And went chasing his tail.

Crusty meanwhile,
On his back in the dirt,
Yelled, "What are you doing?
I might have been hurt!"
    "That's right," whispered Beetle
As he pushed the crab over.
    "Now come with us quick,
Back to Sea Meadow clover."
    "I will not," said the crab.
"Get your feet off of me.
As I told you before,
I don't need you three."
    The fox disappeared
After several more bites;
Experience taught him
Who wins in flea fights.

"Now then," said Fleabus,
Shaking dust from his cap,
"Thanks to me it is safe
If you still want to nap."

Said the crab with a glare,
"You've run off my guide.
I won't see the lights now
Without my free ride."

"You do take the cake,"
Said the flea in disgust.
"If you weren't so stubborn
You'd know who to trust."

"I just thought," said the crab,
"It would be such a pity,
If I came all this way
And then missed the big city."

"There is no big city,"
Said Flutterby firmly.
And the tone of her voice
Made him feel rather wormly.

"Flea saved you," said Beetle,
"From a terrible ride.
Fox only takes riders
From out to inside!"

"And, too," said the flea,
"Since we're speaking of things—
Those bees would have had you
Had it not been for Wings."

Crusty was solemn,
And if they'd had a lamp,
The rest would have seen
That his eyes were quite damp.

Crusty stared at his toes
While a full minute passed.
"Well, it's true what you say,"
Said Crusty at last.
"I'm rude and ungrateful,
And cranky and proud."

He somehow felt better
To say it out loud.

"Forgive my behavior;
Can't I please make amends?
I think I know now
Who to call my true friends."

"Of course, we forgive you,"
Said the other three then.

Crusty might have felt warmer,
But he couldn't say when.

"You've all been so kind,
And your meadow is grand.
But the sea's more for me;
I'm not built for land."

"Well, then," said Beetle,
"We'll lead you back home
To the sound of the waves
And the spray of the foam."

With that, Beetle whistled
And soon all the night
Was filled with the winging
Of millions of lights.

"My Firefly cousins,"
Said Beetle Brightknee,
"Please light the way home
For our friend from the sea."

They turned up their lamps,
Those shining winged bugs,
And they saw a blue crab
Get a butterfly hug.
Then they shone him on home
To the edge of the sea,
Where he lives to this day,
As content as can be.

And now when the tide
Thunders in every day,
Crusty always remarks
How he likes it that way.
And sometimes he catches
A crab leaving town,
And he asks him to stop,
And he has him sit down.
And then over sea tea
Or sometimes some kelp,
Crusty tells his adventure
To be of some help.

"So wait," Crusty says,
"'Til this evening at five,
And meet my good friends
Who are due to arrive."
For Flutterby, Fleabus,
And Beetle Brightknee
Come down every day
For a chat by the sea.

Now when Beetle plays music
The crab hums along
And Fleabus is learning
To sing a whale song.
And Crusty's at home
Under Jaggedy Ledge,
Down by the sea,
By its rippling edge.

Publisher's Note

THE CRANKY BLUE CRAB is a rhymed variation on the adage "The grass is always greener on the other side of the fence." Crusty the Crab, bored and disgruntled, leaves his home in the sea and sets out for the meadow, sure that new surroundings will make him happy. He soon finds that every place has its pains and pleasures and that happiness has more to do with his attitude than with his environment.

Crusty's trip takes him across Sea Meadow, where he makes three new friends. From a good-natured flea he learns enthusiasm, from a musical beetle he learns to enjoy simple pleasures, and from a beautiful butterfly he learns the joy of helping others. Several jarring encounters and a narrow escape from a wily fox make him realize the true worth of his friends and give him a better understanding of what it takes to be content.

Books by Dawn Watkins
The Cranky Blue Crab
A King for Brass Cobweb
Medallion
Jenny Wren